This book is for all of you
who work for a greener tomorrow.
May the wild blue girl always
be at your back.

*The name Poul
is the Danish form of Paul
and is pronounced the same way.*

Balzer + Bray is an imprint of HarperCollins Publishers.
Copyright © 2020 by Keith Negley
All rights reserved. Manufactured in China.
No part of this book may be used or reproduced in any manner whatsoever without
written permission except in the case of brief quotations embodied in critical articles
and reviews. For information address HarperCollins Children's Books, a division
of HarperCollins Publishers, 195 Broadway, New York, NY 10007.
www.harpercollinschildrens.com

Library of Congress Control Number: 2019935928
ISBN 978-0-06-284680-8

The artist used aquarelle pencils, cut paper, and Adobe Photoshop to create the illustrations for this book.
Typography by Dana Fritts
19 20 21 22 23 SCP 10 9 8 7 6 5 4 3 2 1
❖
First Edition

The
BOY
and the
Wild Blue
GIRL

Keith Negley

BALZER + BRAY
An Imprint of HarperCollinsPublishers

There once was a boy named Poul who was curious about everything. But he was especially curious about the wild blue girl.

She liked to swirl through the streets,
making a big commotion.

He liked her straightaway.

She often blew in out of nowhere,

and she didn't always know her own strength.

Everywhere she went,

it seemed she just wanted to help.

But everywhere she went . . .

. . . she really didn't.

Everyone thought the wild blue girl was a nuisance.

Everyone except Poul.

The others couldn't see it, but he knew she was special.

"We just need to show them," he whispered.

Poul loved to study the way things move,
and he wanted to help. After a good bit
of thinking, he had an idea how.

Setting right to work,

he studied and measured,

tested and built.

And as he worked, the town grew curious.

"Poul is making something new,"
they said. "Something different!"

But what could it be?

or as long as a year. Inimitable
s, Detroit, Chicago, Washington,
MR. AND MRS. BUNNEY serve food with an all-Wales
of the
be greater if most of
rnalia be left at home.
is always
and

When he was finally done, he wondered
if the town would now appreciate the
wild blue girl for what she was . . .

. . . and what she did best.

And, happily, they did.

ASKOV.

Prof. Poul la Cour.

This book is inspired by the life of Danish scientist and inventor **Poul la Cour**, who built one of the first electricity-generating wind turbines, located in the town of Askov, Denmark. The turbines depicted in this book are the modern equivalent to what he designed over a hundred years ago.

Born in 1846, la Cour studied meteorology (the science of atmosphere and weather), which led to his fascination with wind. He devoted years to inventing a method of harnessing its energy to produce electricity for farmers who couldn't afford it otherwise. He transformed his windmill into an electric power plant, and by 1902 the village of Askov was lit completely by wind power! The Askov turbine worked all the way up until 1958. After la Cour's death in 1908, other scientists continued his work, and, as of the writing of this book, Denmark has become the most important supplier of wind turbines in the world. Today renewable wind energy is more popular and important than ever, and Poul la Cour's research and designs have become the foundation for modern wind turbines and the hope for a clean, sustainable future.

Special thanks to Bjarke Thomassen and the Poul la Cour Museum for their aid in my research for this book. You can find more information on la Cour and his groundbreaking work at www.poullacour.dk.